A new baby is on the way.
The family is moving out of Number
47 to a bigger house around the corner.
The cat has gone missing. But
everything else is packed and ready
to go.

    Nothing has been left behind. . . .

Orchard Books, 95 Madison Avenue, New York, NY 10016

Manufactured in Hong Kong by Imago
The text of this book is set in 18 point ITC Garamond Light.
The illustrations are watercolor reproduced in full color.
10 8 6 4 2 3 5 7 9

Library of Congress Cataloging-in-Publication Data
Inkpen, Mick.
Nothing / by Mick Inkpen. — 1st American ed.
p.   cm.
Summary: Left behind by the family in whose attic he has been staying, a
thing who has forgotten his name tries to find out who he is.
ISBN 0-531-30076-5 (alk. paper)
[1. Identity—Fiction. 2. Toys—Fiction.] I. Title.
PZ7.I564No 1998 [E]—dc21 97-30898

NOTHING
MICK INKPEN

ORCHARD BOOKS   NEW YORK

The little thing in the attic at
Number 47 had forgotten all about
daylight. It had been squashed in the
dark for so long that it could remember
very little of anything. Stuck beneath
years of junk, it could not recall how it
felt to stand up, or to stretch its arms.
It had been there so long, even its own
name was forgotten.

I wonder who I am,
it thought. But it
could not remember.

The day came when the family that lived at Number 47 was ready to move. All day long the little thing listened to thuds and thumps and the sound of tramping feet in the house below, until at last the attic door was flung open and large hands began to stuff cardboard boxes full of junk.

The little thing felt the weight on top of it gradually lighten, and suddenly the glare of a flashlight beam stung its eyes.

"What have we got here?" said a voice.

"Oh, it's nothing," said another. "Let the new people get rid of it."

The flashlight was turned off. The boxes were carried out. And moments later, somewhere down below, the front door slammed shut. Number 47 was empty.

So that's my name, thought the little thing, Nothing.

For the first time in a very long time, Nothing sat up. He looked around him at the cobwebs and shafts of dusty moonlight. In the quiet he heard the patter of feet, and a mouse came running toward him.

"New People always get rid of you," it said, without introducing itself. It looked at him. "Seen you under the rug. What are you?"

"Nothing," replied Nothing.

"Well, nothing or not, you can't stay here, not with New People coming," said the mouse. It hurried off.

Nothing struggled to his feet. On unsteady legs he followed the dusty paw prints. The mouse stopped by a moonlit gap under the eaves.

"Through there," it said. "Good luck!"

With a wriggle of its tail it disappeared under the floorboards.

I used to have a tail! thought Nothing suddenly. He felt sure of it.

How do you think you would feel if you had been squashed in the dark for years and years? And then you squeezed through a tiny hole to find yourself under the big starry sky?

Well, there are no words for that kind of feeling. So I won't try to tell you how Nothing felt, except to say that he sat on the roof staring up at the moon for a very long time.

He was still staring upward as he made his way along the gutter—which is why he fell straight down the drainpipe!

othing rolled into the garden and sat up.

"What on earth are you?" said a silky voice. A fox—for that is what it was—left the trash can and trotted toward him.

"I'm Nothing," said Nothing.

The fox sniffed at him. Its whiskers quivered. Its ears pricked.

I used to have ears and whiskers! thought Nothing. I'm sure of it.

The fox spoke again. "Nothing," it said disdainfully. "Nothing worth eating, that's for sure." It trotted away silently.

othing wandered into the garden and came across a lily pond. There a frog sat gently croaking. As Nothing approached it plopped into the water, and with a kick of its stripy legs it disappeared from view.

I used to have stripes! thought Nothing. I'm sure I did!

The ripples cleared and Nothing found himself staring at his own reflection. It was odd. It was ugly.

"What are you?" it said to Nothing sadly. A tear rolled up its face and splashed onto the surface of the pond. The ugly face disappeared among the ripples.

"What are you?" repeated Nothing.

I'm a cat!" said a loud voice. "Who's asking?"
A big lolloping tabby cat tumbled out from
behind a bush and grinned at Nothing.

Nothing opened his mouth to explain that
he had been talking to himself, and that he did
not know what he was and that
he was lost, and that he had
just been sniffed by a
horrible fox, and that he
was feeling very miserable.
But instead he found himself
shuddering and shaking, as great uncontrollable
sobs quivered up his raggedy body and sat
him on the ground.

"I don't know who I am!" he howled. "I don't
know who I am!"

The cat licked his face.

After a while
Nothing stopped crying.
The cat lay down
beside him. Between
Nothing's loud sniffs it told him all about
itself. How its name was Toby. And how it
came from a long line of Tobys.

"I live in a house," it said. "At least I
used to. We moved around the corner
today. They think I'm lost. But it's all the
same to me. Number 47, Number 97,
what's the difference? It's all my
neighborhood. Do you want to see?"

Nothing sniffed once more and
nodded.

Of course you do!" said the cat. It picked up Nothing and sprang onto the garden wall.

Nothing had never ridden through the night in a cat's mouth before. The cat whisked him up through the branches of a tree and out onto the rooftops, where they sped along, with the moon racing them behind the chimneys.

"I'm taking you the long way around," panted the cat. "It's more fun."

All the while, joggling along inside Nothing's head, was a thought trying to get out. It felt like an important thought. It had something to do with the cat.

The cat jumped the fence at Number 97 and trotted in through the back door. He found an old man dozing in a chair surrounded by unpacked boxes.

"That's Grandpa," whispered the cat to Nothing, and dropped him on the old man's lap.

"So there you are!" said Grandpa, waking up. "What have you brought me this time?" He put on his glasses and looked at Nothing. "Good heavens! Look everyone! Look what Toby's found!"

Nothing looked up at Grandpa and saw a face he knew. The important thought inside his head popped open like a jack-in-the-box.

The family gathered round to look.

"What is it, Grandpa?" said the children. But Grandpa was busy rummaging among the cardboard boxes.

"I know it's here somewhere," he said. "Ah, there it is!"

He pulled out an old photo album and opened it, turning the pages until he came to a faded photograph of a baby.

"That's me!" he said. "And that's Toby's great-great-great-great-grandfather. And this," he said, tapping the photograph and tickling Nothing's tummy with his forefinger, "this is Little Toby."

At last Nothing remembered who he was. Though he had no ears, nor whiskers, no tail, and no stripes, he was for certain a little cloth tabby cat whose name was not Nothing but Little Toby.

When the new baby arrived, Little Toby was handed back to Grandpa, who tucked him carefully in the cot.

And right away the new baby began to chew on his ear, which, if it had been your ear, would probably have hurt a little, but since it belonged to a little cloth cat, did not hurt in the slightest.

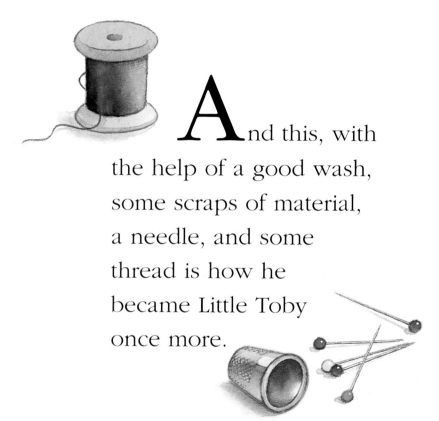

And this, with
the help of a good wash,
some scraps of material,
a needle, and some
thread is how he
became Little Toby
once more.